T0371285

Usborne Dinosaur Tales

The Dinosaurs Who Loved Applause

Russell Punter

Illustrated by Andy Elkerton

Sid needs stars for his big show.

Which dinos might it be?

Omar?

Maisie?

Rory?

Jen?

Or loud twins Gus and Dee?

Sid's show is just one
week away.

Auditions are today.

Gus and Dee stride
right inside.

"The STARS are here!"
they say.

The acts get set to go on stage.

They're waiting in the wings.

"I'll see the first act now," says Sid.

It's Omar's turn to sing.

7

He starts to sing his song,
but then...

Gus and Dee grab
microphones.

Let's take it
from the top!

"Now, you two, wait your turn," says Sid.

"Let Omar sing his song."

The twins stomp off while Omar sings.

Maisie is the next on stage.

But Dee and Gus shove
her aside, before she's had
a chance.

"It's Maisie's turn right now," sighs Sid.

"Well, really!" grumbles Dee.

Sid watches Maisie's lively dance.

That looked just right to me.

Here's Rory with his magic act.

But then, just like before...

Gus and Dee push to the front.

"Let Rory have a try,"
says Sid.

"Well if he *must*,"
gripes Gus.

It's Jen's turn now,
to tell some jokes.

Before she's even tried...

...up rush Dee and Gus once more.

"Oh, *do* let Jen perform," says Sid.

Soon Sid has seen each
act in turn.

Now he must
choose the best.

He lines the winners up
on stage...

and says thanks
to all the rest.

"There must be some mistake," wails Dee.

"We were the stars!" shouts Gus.

35

"You tried to steal the show," says Sid.

"You should let others have a chance."

The twins feel bad.
A week goes by.

They go to see the show.

When they arrive –
there's Sid, outside.

"Rick is sick. He does the lights."

I don't know what to do.

"Well, we can help out,"
Dee declares.

We'll work the lights for you!

"You'll be behind the scenes," says Sid.

"That's quite all right," says Gus.

Curtain up! Unseen by all,
the twins control each light.

Thanks to them, the acts
look great.

The two work hard
all night.

Then Sid calls Gus and
Dee on stage.

"Join in the bows," he roars.

Series editor: Lesley Sims

Reading consultant: Alison Kelly

With thanks to Anne Washtell

First published in 2023 by Usborne Publishing Ltd., Usborne House,
83-85 Saffron Hill, London EC1N 8RT, England. usborne.com
Copyright © 2023 Usborne Publishing Ltd.

Look out for all the great stories in the Dinosaur Tales series!

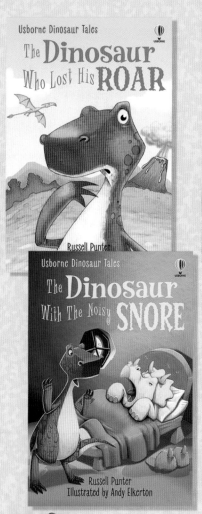

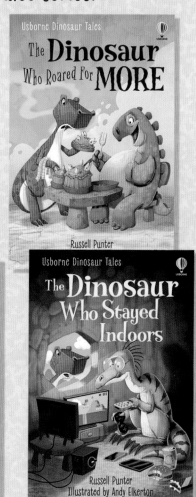

They're totally roar-some!